Frankie's Desires

Feb. / 94

To Bill Latta,

Great to see & hear you
+ don't give up on
that writing!

Best,

Ken Reid

Frankie's Desires

KEN RIVARD

Quarry Press

A number of these Frankie poems appeared in a chapbook entitled *Losing His Thirst* (Pierian Press, 1985). Others appeared in [on]: CBC Radio (Alberta Anthology), *CV/II, Dancing Visions Anthology* (Thistledown Press, 1985), *Poetry Canada Review, Poetry Toronto, Quarry,* and *Skylines.*

This book is dedicated to the author's brother, Bob, and his sister, Diane.

The author wishes to thank The Alberta Foundation for the Literary Arts for a writing grant which helped in the preparation of this book.

The publisher thanks The Canada Council, the Ontario Arts Council, and Alberta Culture for assistance in producing, distributing, and promoting this book.

Canadian Cataloguing in Publication Information

Rivard, Ken, 1947-
    Frankie's Desires

Poems.
ISBN 0-919627-54-4

    I. Title.

PS8585.I82F7 1987   C811'.54   C87-090206-7
PR9199.3.R58F7 1987

Cover design and illustration by Sandy Lynch. Photograph by Don Cope. Typeset by ECW Production Services, Oakville, Ontario. Printed by Tri-Graphic Printing (Ottawa) Limited, Ottawa, Ontario.

Published by *Quarry Press*, Inc. P.O. Box 1061, Kingston, Ontario K7L 4Y5

Contents

Lost Messages

Strange Motives

COMMON PROPS

The Most Common Props

when people call him Frankie
instead of Frank
it sounds like someone is looking
for a tail to wag a dog
and that someone could be a stripper
walking her dog across the stage
they say she likes to use
the most common props in her act

the echo of Frankie has that glide
of a stripper's final performance
but those calling him Frankie
are skeletons in the stripper's audience
who have done time in graves
who are tired of headstones
and are in the process of being moved to museums
because in their plates they begin seeing
right next to the carrots and potatoes
brittle bits of brown reason
right here in this bar

Running Shoe Tree

Frankie prefers running shoes to leather shoes
but dad plus wallet make leather come first

and the next day Frankie's feet take the leather shoes back
to where the clerk lets him trade them for runners
shoes from the leather shoe tree have never been tougher
the clerk tells Frankie with sadness

plucking a pair of running shoes like peaches
from a running shoe tree   the clerk
tells him he'll he happier with these

Frankie wants to grow his own running shoe tree at home
so the clerk snips a cutting
and tells Frankie to plant it only in his bedroom
to never use a leather shoe to water it

Frankie wonders what will happen if his father
decides that a running shoe tree is not practical
but the clerk overhears Frankie's thoughts
by reminding Frankie he's doing all this
for the good of his feet
and if that doesn't work   Frankie should tell his father
the store has plenty of leather in the back

His Sister To Be

while watching tv Frankie hears the front door
open up Frankie   it's me   your sister   someone
is following me   do something   quick
and Frankie grabs his hockey stick
opens the door
quickly slams it   like that tv comedian
then he attaches the chain
rams the back of a chair under the door handle
but the yelling persists and Frankie remembers
he's left the tv on

on the tv he sees a girl being attacked by a strange man
and she looks very much like Frankie's sister
then he remembers his sister is locked out
so he runs to the door   opens it
and she is too undone by fear
trying to get her brother's attention
but it is like catching a passing cloud with a flytrap
and that's how it is with Frankie
that's how he thinks
he wants his sister to be

A Kid Like Him

Frankie's kid brother
in the backyard of the apartment building
wears a cub scout hat above his squint
hides from the camera
between brackets of sun

short pants refuse
to hide his razor blade knees
but the kid brother
so quick in his thinness
appreciates the glare
makes him order his thoughts
place them in a quiet room
keeps his weaknesses private
laughs at weekly cub scout meetings
where the idea of becoming a priest
invades his astonishing mind

he writes letters to prime ministers
and expects replies as a matter of fact
but if he doesn't receive an answer
he stands in the backyard
usually in his cub scout hat
where he asks aloud
why prime ministers are afraid
of a kid like him

Frankie's kid brother will never
make a good boy scout
even though one day
he'll be running this country
still squinting beneath his brain

Words Stumbling

in confession Frankie admits
he touched a girl three times
but the priest doesn't believe him
and Frankie has to say he did it seven times
before he is found credible

as penance Frankie is to stand outside the principal's office
(no kidding) for one hour after school
and Frankie wonders how the priest knows
it was seven and not three
even though he was scared
by the honesty of his own words
stumbling over their own curiosity
accused of withering all they touch
placed there by the telling
of someone else's fortune

When The Kiss Is Real

Frankie wants to kiss a girl   any girl
so he asks a neighbour girl to play husband and wife
and they will pretend their house is on a landing
at the top of the stairs of an old house
abandoned by family years ago

Frankie asks her to pretend he's home from work
she is to kiss him hello   it's been tough at work
he's tried to get a raise

he trudges up the stairs   stops
quickens his pace to kiss his wife hello
after the kiss she moans about their daughter being sick
a call from their son's school pincipal
a blocked washing machine   her headache
but what you need is another kiss   Frankie implores
and he walks downstairs to pretend
he's just come home from work
and what she needs is not in this house

up the stairs runs Frankie
to carve his tongue initials in her mouth
and she is ready to slap him
when she remembers her role
how was your day   she asks
and Frankie is thinking of driving home
again to the land of tv husbands
where life is what happens
when he's making other plans

Harpo Marx and the Catalogue Queen

late at night Frankie is watching *A Day At The Races*
and suddenly Harpo steps out of the tv
scampers towards Frankie
only to sit on his knee

HONK   HONK   HONK
HONK   HONK   HONK

then Harpo sees a department store catalogue nearby
and with slow honks he leafs his way
towards the ladies' wear section
where he lingers over a woman in the latest swim wear
and Harpo is losing control of his honking

then Groucho bounds into the living room
flicking cigar ashes over the rug
the other actors and actresses stop what they are doing
and stare into Frankie's living room
Groucho orders Harpo to give Frankie back the catalogue
so they can get on with the movie
but Harpo pays no attention
his hand now numb from honking
finally Harpo speaks for the very first time
and says he will not leave Frankie's knee
until everyone guarantees
they'll ask the girl in the catalogue
to star in the next Marx Brothers film
but his voice lets Frankie down
because it will always be looking
for that nameless woman of catalogues
that perfect movie queen

Until It Nearly Merges

sometimes Frankie thinks of becoming an altar boy
but quickly palms away the idea because of the exposure
too bad   the most popular guys in school are altar boys
and they never have trouble meeting girls

Frankie can't believe how they remember those altar responses
and every Sunday after church the girls cluster
around those altar boys on the steps outside
as if all holy adolescent boys had it made

today the most popular boy in school is on the altar
so Frankie imagines he's the boy's partner
and they both find time to pray
for Frankie to meet a girl after mass

outside   Frankie watches his shadow being approached
by the most beautiful girl in his class
and she stops on the head of his shadow
is joined by Frankie's pretend altar boy partner
but a large group of kids slowly surrounds them
making Frankie completely lose his own shadow in the crowd

still feeling on the outside   Frankie begins
moving his shadow until it nearly merges
with another belonging to a girl
standing right there on the circle's rim

Not Even with a Mind Mitt

(for Bill Kinsella)

at the game Frankie hopes either he or his father
might catch a baseball
and twice during the action they explode
forwards and backwards   lunging
for white cowhide
no luck

after the game Frankie's father is stopped
by a man holding a nearly new ball
excuse me mister   wanna buy a baseball for your son
only two bucks   caught it in the ninth inning myself
no thanks   Frankie's dad says
it just wouldn't be the same
please Dad   that looks like a game ball   Frankie begs
not the same Son   not the same

at the bus stop they hear the ballseller
excuse me mister   wanna buy a baseball for your son
only a buck and a half   caught it myself in the ninth inning
I don't have a son   replies the man
(but he is ready to buy it anyway)

please buy that baseball before it's too late   Frankie pleads
I can't   we didn't do the catching   says Frankie's dad
then why is that man not afraid to pretend
maybe it's because he doesn't have a son   Frankie

Through His Puffing

behind the giant billboard Frankie is smoking for the first time
and immediately his body wants to leave him   his head
swims in its very own pool

can't take it eh   says one boy
looks like he's zonked   says another

with no safe place to recover Frankie leaves
and glides to the front of the billboard
where the advertisement is for RIDER CIGARETTES   there
a cowboy sits on his horse in a green suede valley
with a long cool RIDER nudged between his lips
and Frankie asks to borrow his horse

now you can still see Frankie
riding back and forth across the billboard
from sunrises to sunsets
trying to forget that first cigarette
and then he will set up camp
in an ideal location
just next to that perfect billboard campfire

Friends and Enemies

Frankie   a puff of combat wind
jumps into a make believe trench   this
is war

with plastic rifle ready Frankie waits
BANG BANG YOU'RE DEAD
a voice behind belonging to his friend
and Frankie rolls over
gets off a final shot
kills the enemy   his buddy
and both boys stop quick movements
to be on the right side of death

for those few seconds when they fake extinction
Frankie wonders how silence can last so long
is asking this question over and over
without blinking an eye
because you never know
when the enemy will become a friend again

In Its Place

(for the kids on Dion Street)

at their fort in the field Frankie sees his friends
chasing a huge rat through the grass   the rat
knifes diameters across its own circles
and is soon smacked out cold by a rock

the rat   tied to a stick   placed
across a fire   listen to the rat's death
listen to the boys running to their fort
and it's Frankie's turn to be lookout on the roof

later at home   Frankie is about to slip into sleep
when he hears that gnawing
behind the baseboard near his bed   tonight
the rats are noisier than usual
and Frankie covers his head with a pillow
so silence will be that wood never burned
and his mind in a place
making a heaven out of hell

Determination

(for Derek)

on a beach Frankie finds a rubber glove
in the flooded rumpus room of his sandcastle
when he gets back to his picnic table
his mother tells him to stop blowing up the glove
that it is not a balloon
and he should go wash out his mouth

after lunch Frankie sneaks off to that glove
and of course first washing out the fingers
then blowing all his determination into the rubber

soon the glove grows   and grows
until Frankie is lifted into the sky
while the resident children of his sandcastle
throw beach balls at him
to help Frankie prove to his mother
that owning such a sky hand
is all there is to this beach
is all there is to this event
brought on by the sun's calculating hum

Night Thumps

(for Donny)

at his friend's rented cottage Frankie cannot sleep
as mice are practising the xylophone on venetian blinds

next night Frankie squeezes 3 in 1 oil on the blinds
and towards midnight he half awakes
to the sounds of tiny base drums
thumping on the floor near the window

in the morning Frankie finds a note
pinned to a corner of his pillow
among other things it reminds Frankie
that musicians only face their fears
when necessary

Laughing Boards

after being checked by the defenceman   Frankie
listens to what he swears is laughter
coming from the boards   later
Frankie again tries to deke the same defenceman
but he is flung into the same laughing boards
with the defenceman smiling over him

third try   Frankie   slammed into the boards
begs the ref to do something
and the referee blows his whistle
points to the boards saying   two minutes for cross-laughter
and the linesman removes the guilty section
piles them tightly in the penalty-box
but it can't just be the boards laughing at him

Frankie   up ice a fourth time
dekes the defenceman   scores
but his move sends the defenceman
into the black hole
where the penalized boards used to be

ref calls time
skates over to the hole
where players begin poking their sticks
but the defenceman is never heard from again
until six months later
when he sends his coach a postcard
explaining how he's now operating
The Idi Amin Hockey School

Pinballs and the Orange Bathing Cap

girl in the pool snaps Frankie's gaze
like a rubber band   in and out of a dream
her rope-brown arms   all of her a beauty
on her head a bright orange bathing cap
which is a beacon for not only Frankie

gradually   very gradually   she slices through chlorine
from the shallow end to the mid-section of the pool
and the water is careful how it laps up against her navel

on his towel Frankie sits watching other boys
paying attention to her in their own ways   see
each is taking a turn diving into the pool
and heading pinball-like to where the girl stands
but just before the underwater silver touches her
it zooms off to the left or right

for a long time Frankie watches
but declines to participate
as she appears to be getting bored
with the water's inconsistent glare

The July Day Begins

you've done this too
you know   wanting to sleep more but work awakes you
far before the splintered day

all night Frankie has been thinking
about a dozen headlines from The Sports Section
what are his favorite hockey players doing this summer
could they be sitting around swimming pools
sipping beer and reliving last year's statistics
but the July morning cool startles Frankie
reminds him that July and hockey don't mix
besides   Frankie has to make a few bucks today
and dreams have no idea of dollars earned

if it weren't for the sun licking its way
up this city's horizon
Frankie would find the day abrasive
but when he thinks of why he's doing all this
he notices that July has its own way
of talking itself out of harsh beginnings

Frankie has three newspaper routes to do each morning
(one hundred and four customers)
makes eighteen bucks a week
enough to soon buy a new bike

as he pedals straight at the sun
Frankie speaks to his vehicle
like others do on their way to work
and it helps him pretend through this day
thinking of that October hockey opener

At the Friday Night Dance

when the slow dance is over
Frankie unglues himself from the girl
and returns to dry-handed games of table-tennis

by concentrating
on the lull of a white ball
Frankie can forget
the rigidity
of his dance steps

after each game   Frankie   his partner
and their two opponents toss their rackets
on the table
sometimes the rackets bear pictures
of certain traditional alllegorical figures
other times the pictures are of actors   actresses   heroes

but if the rackets fall into a pattern
that depicts a certain girl's face
Frankie asks her and only her to dance
and if the rackets happen to look
just like ping-pong rackets
Frankie continues losing himself
in that hypnotic volley
of wood
of white

This Crazy Pain

Frankie dancing with the girl
dancing so so close
as if they are trying
to hide from each other's face
and why does this slow music
bring about the burying of faces
bring on this crazy pain

the girl has two very sharp points
stabbing Frankie in his chest
her bra so big and pointed
and Frankie torn between agony   joy
and the song is three minutes long
but the couple cling
minds elsewhere
helps Frankie forget the pain a little

yes   this slow death dance
body on body
and when the music ends
Frankie will be skewered by the bra
brought somewhere in the sun like game
and what a way to go
two faces never seeing

Whittling in a Lover's Heart

at the skating rink Frankie holds the girl's hand
as they freeze smile their bodies around the ice

something about the girl's hand
allows Frankie to hide his words
the wool of her glove like a shock absorber

they skate together on this Saturday night
feelings woven into each other's grasp
and Frankie wants her
thinks she'll make it all right for him
but with her other hand   her free hand
she motions at the night
draws places of where she'd like to be
who she'd like to be with
while in Frankie's other hand
a fist slowly forms
a fist determined to send enough force
to his occupied hand
shoving his feelings
past the girl's glove
into her free hand
make her empty hand
whittle a lover's heart
on the night-time cold

Elizabeth Taylor and the Strongbox

(circa 1959)

as he leafs through a movie magazine Frankie's wondering
unfolds when he sees Elizabeth Taylor in a bathing suit
he wants to protect Liz by cutting out her picture
and taping it to the outside bottom of his strongbox

next day her husband knocks on Frankie's bedroom door
demanding to know where Liz is hiding
and hubby looks under Frankie's bed   in the closet
    behind curtains
where is she   he demands
no idea   Frankie says
COME ON KID   SHE'S HERE SOMEWHERE
and Frankie lunges at his bureau
to guard the top drawer

she's in your dresser drawer   OUT OF MY WAY
you can't have her   I'm saving her until I'm older
you're crazy KID   bet she's hiding under your clothes
and the husband digs through the drawer finding nothing
you're lucky   he warns   huffing out the door

when he feels it's safe
Frankie opens the drawer whispering   it's ok Liz
he's gone   come on out
thanks Frankie   she breathes
and she removes the tape from her wrists
to slip back to her pose by a swimming pool
on that original magazine page

Why His Gift

two weeks before her birthday
the girl finds she's in love with Frankie
and one week before her party she invites him
and he accepts not feeling too serious
about anything except how to buy a gift

so he buys her a 45 rpm record
and the smallest bottle of Channel No. 5 available
after all it's just another party
for someone Frankie barely knows

at the party the girl opens each present
to the sounds of oohs and aahs
and it's unusual how each expression
is aimed at Frankie standing to one side
and he should be trying to understand
the ever-brightening look in the girl's eyes

now he feels it
knows why his gift
is left until the end
why she looks at him
with more and more anticipation
and Frankie is sliding
into an unwanted celebration

Mouths

Frankie seeking something
watching the tv show
but it is like a force going nowhere
as he kisses the girl harder and harder
and he keeps control of everything else
as if his mouth is used to moderating
all of Frankie's irrational moves

the girl is thinking the same as Frankie
but her mouth is caving in
and so is Frankie's
so they release each other
at precisely the weakest moment
stare at the tv
look for answers in commercials

the tv program continues
and their mouths are back at it
grinding into each other
like that rock
and the hardest of all places
but the closest to a solution
is finding that wall of pain
between their mouths

Genetic Roulette

Frankie wants his ring back from the girl
but he wants to hide the truth
that she has become a mother to him

so he meets the girl
on a busy downtown street corner
safest place to ask for a ring back
and she is relieved
just throws up her hands
hands him the ring
goes back inside the department store
where she works
takes the escalator to the second floor
each steel step
lightens further
the finger that wore Frankie's ring
each steel step
the uncluttered breath
of a woman

Frankie outside
looking for some pain
finds nothing
but the genetic roulette
of being male

Light

there's Frankie sitting
with the creative, serious girl
who only loses control
when she laughs

Frankie is always looking for a match
and it becomes a standing joke
but it's as if he wants to prepare himself
wants her to surprise him

so when Christmas arrives Frankie knows
the girl will give him a present of matches
hopefully in addition to something else
and it happens
when he opens his gift
there is the biggest matchbook
Frankie has ever seen
(plus a butane lighter of course)

there must be a simple creative way
in knowing how to hide your surprise
in knowing how to make your way
through a moment as innocent as now

Doing Time in the Great Outdoors

on the ski trip Frankie and the girl decide
to just sit in the lounge all day
as both their pasts tell them
downhill skiing is usually for the rich

so they plan to sit
watch skiers carve up the slopes
as if the same sheets of paper
were being forever shredded in the sun
and Frankie and the girl will pretend
to have fun if they have to
maybe even go along with expert skiers
by asking about the novice skiers
slipping cautiously down the bunny slopes

Frankie and the girl sip
sloe gin in the afternoon
get up   sit   go outside
think about renting a toboggan
decide it's too cold
go back inside
warn the resting skiers
about a new nip in the air

heading back home on the evening bus
Frankie and the girl are exhausted
from doing time today
with that fashionable outdoor madness
that lounging-about excitement

Dials

Frankie in his basement kissing
the friend of his cousin
who has slept over
she in a nightgown
only awake for a half hour
he with his left hand
slipping down the small of her back
ah this morning kiss
makes Frankie not sure
if it will lead to more
but he is content with his left hand
slipping in and out of that small place

all of this is a holding pattern
as the wings that are Frankie's fingers
stay in their runway grooves
grind like real motors
whine like the winds which are never right
as the line-up of aircrafts just waits
shimmering in the early sun
yes   the planes are covered with epidermis
and pilots sit in the white of each knuckle
their instrument dials threatening
to shatter all time zones

Bumps

Frankie and two buddies
in a downtown bar
watching erotic dancers

the first two performers are female
while all the rest are males
dressed up as women
and Frankie doesn't feel quite right

HOW WOULD YOU LIKE A DATE WITH HER
one of the guys asks Frankie
pointing to the fifth dancer
and the two friends who are in on this scam
shake the table with laughter
tell Frankie about this place

but Frankie pretends he knew all along
only men have Adam's Apples   he thinks to himself
and each dancer from number three on
had that familiar throat bump

the three leave at Frankie's request
stop at a restaurant
and Frankie finally heads to the men's room
where for the first time that evening
he is not looking over his shoulder

LOST MESSAGES

There Are Messages

1.

in his briefcase there are messages
Frankie must deliver
so he puts on his tan plastic raincoat
huddles out into the rain
where humidity is thicker
than the leather of his briefcase
where heat traps itself next to his skin
and the envelopes will need no saliva

the more buildings Frankie walks into
the more the heat takes over his skin
and when the last message has been dropped off
Frankie becomes the center of that wetness
so he runs outside only to feel the rain has stopped

on the way back to the mailroom Frankie peels off the coat
allows the heat to lift from him
sits on a wet park bench
and the air smells
like it just came back from the dry cleaners
but Frankie stuffs the coat into his empty briefcase
as it is time to get back
the head messenger will wonder
what Frankie has done in the rain

2.

Frankie   the youngest there
and the others retired from previous jobs
like the oldest messenger   a retired cop
taking himself very very seriously
tells Frankie to be more conscientious
while Frankie reminds him to stop
behaving like a toothache

often this toothache paces the mailroom floor
as if searching for a lost letter
and Frankie asks another messenger about this guy
is told the man probably spent most of his shifts
patrolling the railroad yards
and watching those wooden ties
so he wouldn't trip

there is no sense in calling him a toothache anymore
as Frankie is starting to understand the pain
and he will let the guy rehearse
the only lines he knows
about the sanctity of work
or the unbending rules of time

3.

whenever a woman walks into the mailroom
the other messengers all look at Frankie
to see if he will react
and Frankie   just nineteen
not so sure of himself with women
but the other messengers want his eyes
to grow up in a hurry

today a young woman walks in
and Frankie's ribs receive three different elbows
when she's gone the men tease Frankie
about being man enough to ask her out
and while the room jumps with laughter
Frankie tries to think of clever things to say
but the noise makes his brain
work at low efficiency

late that night Frankie imagines
asking the girl out
and when she accepts he discovers
she's sexiest when laughing
at those other messengers
in their strange world of elbows

4.

his cheeks are STOP signs
eyes are road maps to intersections
where all signs are made
he is also the best mail sorter and messenger
but the head messenger warns Frankie
to stay away from him
especially when out delivering messages
as his loneliness stories
will cover you from head to toe

later on a street corner
Frankie meets that messenger
and they are in a tavern for a quick one
almost immediately the STOP sign cheeks become redder
on his face because he wants Frankie to laugh along
when he speaks of his own loneliness
(imagine laughing at such a thing)
but Frankie is losing his thirst
before it can develop
anything resembling a smile

5.

messages are slow today
so Frankie is sent to work with the photocopier
and he likes to make this man laugh
but Frankie is shown pictures of a wife   four children
time for Frankie to make copies of his own face
so features can be compared

Frankie   listening to the photocopier's French accent
and he wants to practise big English words on Frankie
in that room of clicking and flipping
but an accountant from the Estates and Trusts Department
asks the photocopier for ten copies of a will
so he can give each person in his family
something different on his birthday

the photocopier   now ignoring Frankie
pressing that button   making copies
and forgetting his own wife and children
as he hums to himself
his favorite French ballad

Before Power Is Restored

at the moving and storage company Frankie finds himself
eternally filing and running messages
so to shatter this haze
he dreams of the receptionist
being half her age
and having her eye on him

one day Frankie and the receptionist
alone in the stockroom looking for supplies
and it happens   a power failure
Frankie   she says   find your way to the door
(silence)
FRANKIEEE   I know you're there
(more silence)
then she begins to feel his look
curling through the darkness
as it wraps itself around her waist
she yells   WHAT DO YOU THINK I AM FRANKIE
SWEET SIXTEEN AND NEVER BEEN KISSED
(lots more silence)

Frankie slips out
before power is restored
walks briskly to the men's room
sits on the hard of a toilet seat lid
repeatedly slams his right fist
into the palm of his left hand
until the receptionist is her real age again

When the Moving Company is Scholarly

1.

just before negotiations for a new contract
Frankie sees the union steward
joking with the company president
so Frankie smiles too because he knows
the two men are trying to con each other

the president reminds Frankie
that he doesn't have to work overtime
if he doesn't want to
and the union steward slaps Frankie on the back
telling him to go home   relax

Frankie is not sure how negotiations have gone
and he's too tired to ask
but he wonders about the two men
giving each other's wallets a break
and the conning reminds Frankie
of a wheelchair man in church
tapping his heels
waiting to confess
a long list of sins   the priest
and his own higher learning
not knowing which side to be on

2.

Frankie   afraid   the three hundred pound man wants him
but dishes should be packed   pictures and mirrors crated
and often Frankie has to look over his shoulder
'cause he knows what the big man wants
and the size of the flesh makes Frankie move fast

he says he likes the way Frankie thinks
and Frankie tells him he's full of it
have you ever heard of de Maupassant   he asks Frankie
JUST LEAVE ME ALONE
OR I'LL SLASH THIS WARDROBE RACK
STRAIGHT ACROSS YOUR FACE
and the huge man stops eyeing Frankie in that way
then lowering his look to the floor
the big man speaks of how his wife
burned to death five years ago
but Frankie dares not pity him

and it happens again
he moves in on Frankie as if wrapping him in tissue
wants to take Frankie home in a china barrel
but as the giant lunges at the last moment
Frankie grabs a hammer and screams
I'LL SMASH YOUR DAMN SKULL
IF YOU COME ANY CLOSER
ENOUGH   YOU HEAR ME   ENOUGH
and Frankie leaves the room
goes outside to help the driver load
starts feeling like a kid wearing earmuffs
half-hiding behind a bag of groceries
on the coldest of all winter days

3.

the forklift driver's voice grows deeper
as he weaves through the warehouse
if his voice and truck were
dropped off a cliff simultaneously   his speech would hit
the ground before his forklift truck
and he is always throwing something somewhere
bolts   balls of string
as if he were always warming up for that one game
today he brakes hard where Frankie is unloading a truck
tells him to bring in a baseball glove tomorrow

next day at lunch   Frankie and the forklift operator
firing a baseball at each other in the yard
and with each successive pitch
the operator increases his speed
is putting on that show of failed athletes

pitch after pitch smacks into Frankie's glove
until Frankie stands
curses the smoke in his glove
thinks of teaching the operator a lesson
but yells at the sun
those high-pitched words
those habits at noon

4.

the nervous driver has pills for everything
and when Frankie is assigned to him as his helper
the driver is happy because he doesn't have to teach
and he hates having outside laborers

but today the third man besides Frankie
is outside help
and the driver grinds into an ugly mood
because ten thousand pounds has to be loaded
time for another pill

on the way to the job the driver
tells the outside laborer his kind are lazy
that all HIS KIND ever do is work just enough
get paid   get drunk   miss work
and Frankie feels the coming of fists

the outside laborer asks the driver
to please pull over
climbs out
and before slamming the door
the most thought-out middle finger
you could ever imagine
but the driver just grunts
says he feels better already
gulps down a yellow capsule

5.

the other helper young and brilliant
tells Frankie of his special scholarship
to begin this autumn
and the scholar tries so hard for perfection
when working with Frankie
when packing customer's effects into cartons

trouble is he can't tie a decent knot
and the boxes stay loose
so Frankie tells him to stop reasoning out
every twist of the twine

on the packing job today
with Frankie working twice as hard as the scholar
because the scholar takes double the time to fill a box
and he reminds Frankie he's only being careful

each china piece is wrapped so carefully
you'd think tissue had a real value in life
but maybe the scholar is right
maybe Frankie should stop
to learn about tissue and glass

Flowers and the Lease

she loves the presence of flowers
and they appreciate her love
but Frankie overhears two workers in the office say
that all she really needs is a job
where flowers can grow without being picked

when there are no flowers on her desk
she is never at work
and when she is sick
she is actually out shopping
so she can feel better

today she is sitting at her flower-less desk
it is that time to check her new apartment lease
so she asks Frankie to check the fine print
been doing that for eight years
for as long as she's been with this company
and every year she asks someone new
so Frankie agrees to go with her because he knows
there'll be fresh flowers on her desk tomorrow

Tar and the Day

Frankie likes to think
the work crew can't see him watching them   five men
are getting ready to plug another pothole   the workers
hardly speak to each other   two
are smoothing out tar   another
directs traffic   a fourth
sits in a truck   the fifth man
prepares oncoming vehicles
nearly a block before the pothole in question

Frankie pretends to be a foreman from far away
and he blames the tar for the lack of conversation
because tar brings everything to a slow pour
and when a hole is being filled with black
it would rather not talk about it

as Frankie gets closer to the hole
he hears himself as foreman
telling the youngest of his crew
IF YOU WANT A LONG AND HEALTHY LIFE
AND BE ABLE TO TALK ABOUT IT
GO TO BED THE SAME DAY YOU GET UP

and for the rest of the day the youngest crew member
can't stop himself from checking
the position of the day
above the growing black patch

Want Ad Safety

not knowing what to do with his vitality   Frankie
drifts into the morning Want Ads   first he
becomes an accountant who is very serious
about those ledger numbers   the figures
intrigue him and he asks the ledger
to send him an invoice
for using up part of its time

then Frankie becomes a truck driver   his vehicle
is being driven by an urge of Frankie's
and the urge is dressed just right in overalls

as a security guard   Frankie
sees himself patrolling with an empty gun
and lots of self-confidence

standing behind a grill   the short order cook
looks at Frankie in the mirror   the cook
is starting to lose his hair
and his hands are never quite clean enough
but he is happy

still sitting on the street curb
and reading The Classified Section
Frankie decides it's far easier
being someone else

Worm Pickers

(for Phil)

STAGE ONE:

Frankie and Friend ripping apart earthworms
and the soil seems to say   only sissies do that
but they are only worms waiting to die in different ways

as Frankie runs into his kitchen to explain new worm surgery
he trips over a rug   a chair's leg slicing through his chin
MY CHIN   IT'S BLEEDING LIKE CRAZY
come and lie down Son   just a cut   his mother says
but before she phones the doctor she asks Frankie
what he's doing with half a worm in his fist

STAGE TWO:

twenty years later very late at night
Frankie climbs into a truck of worm pickers
and they are driven to a golf course
where Frankie meets his worm squeezing friend
who is dressed in all white
what are YOU doing here   he asks
and I see you still have that scar on your chin
would you believe that just last year
I was playing golf on this same course
but before Frankie can respond the foreman shouts
TIME TO GET TO WORK GUYS
and Frankie would rather talk
about his scar

every worm picking leg has a bucket attached to it
on the right leg   a bucket for sawdust and worm slime
on the left leg   a bucket for worms
and as the night ages the men even more
the moon bathes the worms making the job harder

and Frankie's boyhood friend yells
ONLY MEN WHO HATE THEMSELVES
WOULD PICK WORMS FOR A LIVING

Basement Suite

moved here from the capital last year
used to be an ad manager for Pepsi
made good bucks   two cars
new house   top of the line appliances
until payments measured his sanity
time he told management what to do with the job

had to get work as a security guard
watching embassies   hundred hour weeks
hardly seeing his wife and son
at home he's on the bottle
moves out west alone
as wife and son leave

brings one sports jacket
one pair of pants for work
wears turtlenecks only
works as recreation director
eats once a day at nine p.m.
keeps food in someone else's fridge
does laundry in someone else's washer and dryer
drinks room temperature beer
tells Frankie it's easier
in this rented basement suite
asks Frankie what he thinks
of the giant bottle cap of cloud in tonight's sky
but before Frankie can answer
says it reminds him of a soft drink ad
he once knew so well

As a Prelude

(for Ivan)

Frankie's friend   in and out of jobs
never worries too much
thanks Frankie and others
for supporting his habit
is so comical
Frankie feels no anger

whenever he does work
does it so hard and fast
you'd think he was born for labor
but his sweat is measured just enough
to receive unemployment
or he'll take a wage cut
if dollars are under the table

not like other men
who dress up each day
go look for work   pretend
read newspaper stories about themselves

looks out his kitchen window at his neighbor's wife
as they both wash morning dishes
picks up the mail saying HELLO
to the occasional other woman
thinks of inviting the same woman in for coffee
takes his infant son to the park
meets more women   the occasional man
soon there are ten children
following him to the playground

floats on crests of depression
like a tired surfer (his simile)
wishes all workers well
continues watching news
waits for the announcer's optimism
but sees it all as a prelude to retirement
or as an intermission
and Frankie likes his laugh
aimed at those who accuse him of laziness

As Big as the Main Counter

Frankie's Grandpa Joe   home from work
houseful of daughters
spoke of delivering coal
how he didn't have the heart
to force customers to pay

Frankie's Aunt May   home with a box of Shaw's chocolates
best candy in those days
shared the sweets with family
had the warmest look about her too
helped Grandpa Joe forget coal

Aunt Irene   hairdresser
Aunt Lilian   cashier/bookeeper
both worked in The New York Hairdressing Salon on
        Drummond Street
just above St. Catherine in downtown Montreal
catered to society people such as The Molson's
sometimes received jewelry as birthday gifts
and once Grandpa Joe brought home a chunk of coal
just to remind the girls of other issues

Frankie's favorite   Aunt Dorothy   secretary
to the president and vice-president of a large store
came home from work exhausted
three people were hired to replace her when she had child
used to say Aunt Dorothy had a heart
as big as the counter on the main floor

Frankie's mother   C.P.R. secretary
liked the variety of her work
made sure to let everyone know she was home
sprinkled her day around the supper table

Frankie's father   Alcan clerk for twenty-nine years
almost rushed in through the front door
tossed his newspaper onto a chair
removed his suit   tie   put on old pants   faded shirt
slumped into that chair of his
how was your day
how was school
responses seldom varied
funny how he came home
newspaper folded in that accordian way
nobody else could ever put it together again
like the hours of his particular day

Frankie   home from work
imagines away his day
wants his energy
to not be like animals
smacking into fences

STRANGE MOTIVES

Man Frankie/Boy Frankie

tonight Frankie sees himself on tv
and he is a grownup
going back to his childhood
to see where his anger originates from

as soon as he's there
sees himself as a boy
burying a toy soldier in a field
sees himself stealing the soldier
from a platoon on a toy store shelf
but Man Frankie stares at Boy Frankie
and the soldier is put back

when Boy Frankie is picked on by a bully
it is always Man Frankie who saves him
and soon Boy Frankie and Man Frankie
become close   like family
but Frankie's father becomes jealous
wonders what Man Frankie is hiding
and there is a certain rage
in the father's voice

Man Frankie has seen enough
wants to go back to his real place in time
but Boy Frankie wants to go with him

it's impossible   says Man Frankie
and Boy Frankie screams
THEN YOU WERE HIDING
HOW YOU REALLY FELT ABOUT ME

From Talking About It

next door to Frankie   a man and woman
want to have child   any child

find a birth mother
pay her many dollars
hold the man's sperm
beginnings of care
worry about authorities
declaring it all illegal

many couples are desperate
for the smell of child
but the birth mother idea
keeps people from talking about it
keeps it all right here

the couple will take the infant
even if it has a defect
yes   even if they split up
they are so prepared
Frankie asks no questions

they will not even force the birth mother
to give up the child
should she decide to keep it
and an agreement
between a childless couple and birth mother
could be enforceable
if allowed
they may resort to adopting the same baby
creating domino sets
their own rules

Frankie tries to understand
their preparation for child
but the falling rain
is shredding the truth

For the Headache Brought On

he is the smallest ever born
just fourteen ounces
almost entered the world
when his mother stood up after urinating

lives in the hospital for five days
kicks and squirms his way
through the possibilities of living

the day before his death
Frankie is able to understand him
tells Frankie of his horror
of being born before his time

right now the infant
is making up suicide riddles for Frankie
is refusing most drugs
for the headache brought on
by his thinking

Big J

Frankie's neighbor   Big J
believes his phone is being tapped
is being watched by a man across the street
who measures time in a wheelchair

next door to the wheelchair peeper
a policeman lives   maybe watching Big J too
but Big J swears he has never stolen
has nearly quit most of his habits

Frankie imagines Big J being arrested
for biting a chunk from the moon
and Big J's sentence
is to glue each flower he has snipped
back to the original stem

when Frankie asks Big J how he knows
someone is watching him
Big J says   I started using my own binoculars
and saw the cripple getting ready to study me

Over Coffee and Doughnuts Only

(for Lorraine)

man next to Frankie
has for years asked the same woman out
takes her to church
both confess sins
receive communion
back to her place
for coffee and doughnuts
and thus begins the pattern

when they marry
both remind Frankie
no booze in their home
no need to loosen tongues
tighten brains
outings are now
nightly prayer and meditation
over coffee and doughnuts only

plan on children   Frankie asks
but they want to be debt-free
don't want their child
in the world as it is
don't care if it's a boy or girl
as they'll teach the child
what has brought them
so far in their own lives

The Hospital's Glass

inhale   exhale   inhale   exhale
man in the bed beside Frankie
is a breathing machine
and a stomach tube helps the man
live the sounds of a cold water tap
turned on dripping forever

a patch of right lung is gone
removed like a price tag
but the wound on his back won't heal
doctors saying he has to eat

visitors call him grandpa or dad
a tv hanging by a ceiling rod is a glass ear
listening to the man's son
speak of January sales at Canadian Tire
and the man smiles at Frankie
after hearing his son's notion of deals

the timid son
turns off the cold water tap   his father's lungs
need to try it on their own
and Frankie is asked how he'll like the silence
the only get well gift left behind
as the man and his family head to the visitor's lounge
next day a man and woman visit
the woman gasping like a garden hose
out of control
climbed one hundred and eighty five steps with her husband
as elevators always open up fears

Frankie   down being X-rayed
sees a cigarette burning in an ashtray
behind the wicket where he leaves his doctor's request
the technician   complaining how her lipstick
smudges the filter   changes the taste

Frankie   in the recovery room
shivers   trembles out of control
more blankets   he pleads
the nurse telling him to breathe deeply
get his circulation going
now Frankie making so much breathing noise
the machines sound as if they don't work

another patient sees Frankie in the lounge
asks him for a game of cribbage
says he's been here for nineteen weeks
didn't eat for fifteen weeks
lost fifty pounds
maybe you heard   he says
got hit in the belly with a shotgun blast
and doctors predict they'll never be able
to remove all the pellets

Cages to Sell

man at the corner speaks
through his earnest look
to Frankie   on the man's lap
an open suitcase containing birds in tiny cages
birds for sale   cage included
tells Frankie he'll sell all
later use the suitcase
to store vegetables
in the cool dark below his kitchen floor

the man sprinkles powder in his bird feeder
so birds soon fall asleep
are placed in cages to sell

birds that do not wake
are used as fertilizer in his garden
and last week for the first time
noticed carrots and their green tops
as an utterance

Where Rust is Born

black-bearded white man points to a field
filled with abandoned cars
tells Frankie they must belong to Native Indians

who else   he says   would drive into nowhere
allow decay in a place
where rust is born
before it hits the ground
who else   his weakening voice seems to say
will always be outside my blood   blood
filled with abundant oxygen
but thinning with time

his words now lower than a whisper
are now coming
from the mouth of a starving child
thousands of miles from here
a child too weak to cry
or justify the loneliness of vehicles

Requesting the Death Penalty

the killer once requested the death penalty
later changed his mind
is still on death row
tells Frankie his execution could take place
from eighteen months to ten years from now

if he hadn't changed his mind a year ago
he could have died last summer
but there has been no execution here since 1943

hitching rides from Calgary to Mexico
shoots two men for their car   no witnesses
and when Frankie studies the killer's eyes
he is not sure who is behind them

wants to be locked away from life and death
as he has become that parrot
who does not want to learn to speak
or ever leave the cage

Sinks

with his face in the bathroom mirror
Frankie's hands rub his temples
and the booze glow is a reckless fire
scorching red roads
on the whites of his eyes

then his hands slip down to the sink
and he can't hide his face from himself
from his weight
which is tugging the sink from the wall
time for Frankie to stumble outside
cling to a steel fence
empty his stomach at the moon

at home Frankie is soon
a deadened heap on his bed
and behind his eyes a wall of sinks
keeps falling on him
and he cannot stop the revenge of the moon
because the vomit is trying to re-enter his mouth
and his hands are back at his temples
temples racing with his sleep
to see who dies first
just before dawn a winner is announced
and it is not Frankie
because when he awakes
the sinks are dropping
faster and faster

When Rose Petals Need Not Bite

he is half-way between anger
and watching those slow freight trains
rumble through his privacy

tells Frankie he will not tear down
the wall of roses on his front lawn
as the flowers are quiet
aren't ugly
aren't hurting anyone
and if the city wants the wall down
do it themselves

for weeks nothing more
the roses grow larger than ever
their smell takes over the street
and Frankie feels they are covering the man's hostility
with that sweet-smelling religion
and whatever city objections remain
now just confuse themselves
it happens that way
when rose petals need not bite

The Scenery is Hidden

right to the end he keeps working
as teeth grind away pain
children ask all those questions

falls into a coma last Friday
at what he considers the muscled age of forty-eight
awakes Monday morning
wonders why Frankie and everyone else
are standing near his bed
is disappointed he didn't die before Chistmas

death is like a car doing ninety in the fog
but everything appears slower
because the scenery is hidden in white   he says

asks for a cigarette
smokes it
wants a big party at his funeral
and five minutes later   dead

dies on Monday at eight a.m.
in the funeral parlor for three days
at the church a real party
singing   guitars   one violin
five cars of flowers to the cemetery
windows rolled down
radios on full blast
all listening to the top ten hits
there on Thursday
that warm Christmas week

Frankie Clapping for Fifteen

1.

young girl   her sweater is her training bra
plays piano as if her fingers pluck strings

2.

clenches her music book
peeks at the back row
glances at her notes
winks at her punk rock body
playing classical

3.

a rainbow drips across her chest
breathes behind her black dress
bites her lip between verses
and her eyes out-blue the sky outside

4.

woman   hair like rust
wants her music in a story
wants it read forever

5.

because of her melon breasts
Frankie imagines her with child
and her music is a car in heavy traffic

6.

a man with bones too big for his skin
lets the music control his wrists
and his knuckles are boned in harmony

7.

dressed to her bottom lip in white
touches the piano like a nurse with patients
looks for her own cup of warm milk when done
helps the music sleep better in her head

8.

a large Chinese girl
quick beyond the borders of age
has planned all her mistakes
the silence

9.

tiny girl
her very first words were broken chords
mother and father memorizing each note

10.

the high school boy is a basketball forward
size twelve runners
white shirt   tie   suit
plays at the speed of his best shot

11.

never will she be a cheerleader
makeup is not for her face
as her music won't allow it

12.

forty year old woman
sings with an absolute voice
makes the clock's hands disappear

13.

ten year old boy
his fingers sound as if they were placed
before he was conceived

14.

barelegged woman
in charge of her words
in charge of clapping
the beauty inside
the beauty she has a right to

15.

woman of twenty
hands cupped like a choir girl's
releases opera behind her pink dress
hands rotate slightly
pushing out notes from the bottom of her rib cage
is so professional
watch her squeeze the diamond
on her right hand
as she sings without music

Remember the Numbers

she gives cash to sailors
in return for watches and fur hats
in return for time and feelings

is a mixed blessing to Frankie
helps men lose their despair
and under her pawnshop Frankie sees
a watery passageway with face-filled boats

face one is hairless and inward
dimpled with a welt of second chins
has more than furs to sell

face two is explosive and comical
been selling his watch for years
laughs about costs

face three is fisted skyward
on the fringe of a neck
wants more for his money

Frankie is asking you the customer
did you see any sunshine
when you finally remembered
that pawn ticket number
did your mother recall your drowning
the last time you understood
the pawnbroker's symbols

alone in her shop with Frankie
she asks why he has nothing to pawn today
but he says he needs to swim
through her passageway
one more time
to find that lost ticket
that cure

Motives Are Strange

at the back of the church stands Frankie
four rows from the altar a woman on her knees
whispers to a statue
and Frankie walks up to the pew behind her
slides right in

she stops the quickness of her words
turns and flips through a booklet
we're lucky to have a place like this   she says
that's for sure   Frankie says

later at the entrance over pamphlets
Louise and Frankie introduce each other
speak of prayer and reasons for it
but her motives are strange to Frankie
as she prays to be conned
because she feels she's immune
and is desperate for a risk

asks if he is ever vulnerable
and he stops
smells the candle wax
thinks of speaking
tries to pray
forgets the words

Campground Magic Show

(for Annie and Melissa)

Frankie watches birds explode
as if they are flung back at the sky
for their own protection
but Frankie's daughter sees it all
as a curtain for a magic act

the grey eye of the burning log
belongs to a magician
hiding rabbit bones in a fire
and burying gopher ashes
to distract the audience
watch the magician's eye warn Frankie
to beware of the rage
that sleeping hit-list
of failed tricks

a tap on the head from the magician's baton
and Frankie looks up
sees another trickster from the south
tug a northern blanket across the sky
while a novice magic man
looks in garbage cans for empty bottles
but Frankie's daughter explains it all
as the simplicity of a day
running faster than any magician
so not to be discovered

Semblance

birds are gossiping in confusion
asking where all the roaring is coming from
and Frankie looks at the road
sees nothing but pickup trucks
as if a person driving any other vehicle
is unfaithful to the road

in each truck a baseball cap
gunning gear noise at the birds
cassette perched on ashtray
a German Shepherd in the back
and drivers horselaughing
at startled creatures

in reply the birds warn Frankie to hide
and they become firefighters drinking from hoses
after a long fire

look how the wings line up in sky
chaining themselves to the noise
and Frankie hears the birds' plan
to banish these pickup drivers
to their semblance of honor
by flapping in unison
the noise right back

Standing on the Color Near Radium, B.C.

(for Don)

the cavity is stopped dead on the highway
and Frankie stands on loamy color
watches green on white on brown
beyond the camera's rim

where is the bottom half
of this question mark road going
don't let the shade fool you
and watch that guardrail
it has no purpose
rounding the bend

see that postcard sky
it knows all the numbers
will suddenly paint itself
with the craziest brush gasps imaginable

this is the only picture for Frankie
taken by a jagged eye
this is the only picture
taken by a gentle savage
heaped as a handful of sun
near a sky seam

Juan De Fuca Water Ropes

(for Don)

Frankie sees water swelling enough
to begin the coiling of new rope

a seagull shows
how to survey invisible operations
for the lassoing of salmon
for grey sky anchors
for guide ropes of ghost ferries

white holes carved in atmosphere
are the beginnings of a faraway storm
and that's it
are not the results of whiplashed rope tips
from west coast cowboys
who keep repeating to the strait and Frankie
they are sorry for life line delays

The Oregon Ocean is Many Persons

(for Don)

a giant foot was left there
before calendars could roll tides and numbers
before your very eyes

now the foam is white only pages
remind Frankie the foot is a story
heard so often before
watch Frankie standing on the toe
of an even older foot
trying to feel the rationale of moss

the ocean is many persons
one of them the self-conscious giant
who once upon a time had but one foot
but now the hugeness is balanced on two stubs
and foam washes imaginary toes

yesterday the giant was seen belly-up
floating on ocean
and you'd swear he was giggling
at the way Frankie knew
about clear water swirling
below where feet once were

Montreal Canadiens Scout

in Frankie's sleep he is the only
Montreal Canadiens talent scout
and the number one defenceman is hurt
so it is Frankie's job to go down
to the minors for a replacement

Frankie in a small town dining room
filled with minor leaguers
would-be rookies
washed-up veterans
and the word is out
one day to find a replacement

soon Frankie is surrounded by hockey players
casually inquiring about the injury
but Frankie just wants his breakfast
and the morning meal smells
begin to overwhelm him
as his plate is forever being filled
with pancakes   bacon   eggs   sausages
and the crowd grows
becomes the urgings of parents
in a minor league arena

Both Horns

when Frankie is with the possibility
of a new friendship he is afraid
because the chance just performs
for those three to four hours
and after that who knows

what is it
is Frankie too intense or open
and it is starting to not matter
as he is tired of blaming himself

from now on
when Frankie meets the likelihood of a friend
he will survive
digest bad with good
become a Japanese suicide pilot
attending his own funeral before that final flight

afterwards he will use anything
to help him sleep
and let fate overtake things
before his brain goes to his head
before he is skewered
on both horns of his dilemma

Frankie the Snake Oil Salesman

(inspired by a newspaper story)

Frankie back in 1900
among patent medicine pedlars
hawks potent miracles
in dusty frontier towns

flogs Doctor Morse's root pills
and Chief Two Moons bitter oil
even Lydia Pinkham's tincture is used
for all that ails women
and Frankie's best buy is alcohol-laced Indian oil
best to revive the weakest cowboy

on a quiet day Frankie's partner tries out spiels
listen to this
a combination collar buttoner and ear spoon
only 10¢ and a must for the twentieth-century
        well-dressed man
one end of the two inch device buttons clip-on collars
without bending or breaking or soiling them
while the ear cleaner on the other end
is made to the right proportion
to use and not injure the ear
some of Frankie's sales friends take advantage
of the mystique surrounding Indian oils
use the highly costumed natives
to attract townspeople
and when the show hits town it's a big deal

but as the first advertisers Frankie and his cohorts
are also the first to use deception (according to historians)
but Frankie believes in some of his cures
while the others make exaggerated claims
about the medicinal qualities
of laxatives and baking soda
concocted in buckets

Frankie's beard is cut below his cheeks
in turn-of-the-century style
is begging to believe his past
is playing himself into the hands
of a lifetime deal

With Clear Instructions

Frankie's father a senior citizen
receives a request for money
and an oil packet

but Frankie has read
about the evangelist who sends packets of salad oil
resembling vinegar packets from fast-food joints
and are labelled BIBLE ANOINTING OIL
turns out that a half million seniors received these packets
asking them to bless their money with it
send the evangelist the biggest cheque or dollar bill
and they are promised financial blessings
if each of them marks a cross with the oil
on their paper money or cheque
then sends it to the evangelist
and the greater the sacrifice the greater the blessing

some seniors feel obligated to send their biggest cheques
their pension cheques
and they worry about eating for the next month
but the scriptures say to give as you can
and there is nothing suggesting
Frankie's father has to give up food
Frankie's father will keep eating
will keep the salad oil
and send a McDonald's vinegar packet
back to the evangelist
with clear instructions
about the many uses of vinegar

That Heart of Sundown Meat

the evening sky is making Frankie feel
like a man educated beyond his intelligence

the sun   slipping behind sky flesh
pieces torn from the bones of that day
pieces ripped from the skeletons of common creatures
pieces pared from the thighs of orange queens
and Frankie's legs respond
as if they are growing from the feet on up
aiming for a heart
a heart of yellow feasts
that heart of sundown meat

since Frankie has learned beyond his brain
he is left standing
over-analysing the cut-up sky
a sky that keeps on educating itself
beyond the art of cunning

His Position on the Function of Sleep

today the world has finally eaten its way
through the flesh of Frankie's morning
he stands alone in a swimming pool
thinks about pinballs
sees himself in the pool
where on top of the blue-green quiet
there are no shapes

remembers his daughter
who after being awake for an hour this morning
asked to go back and finish her sleep
her own perfect tête-à-tête

beneath the water there are many shapes
wanting a place to go
a place to play
watch them
weave their way to the top   disappear
weave their way to the top   disappear
like a surge of applause
and Frankie wants to stand and bow
so everyone will remember
where he stands